Disney · PIXAR
INSIDE OUT

FEAR

by **Brittany Candau**
illustrated by **Jerrod Maruyama**

DISNEP PRESS
Los Angeles · New York

H-hello!

I'm Fear.

I consider every day we don't die a success.

Especially since the world is full of terrifying things.

Look!
I have a list!

There's the stairs to the basement . . .

**and Grandma's
vacuum cleaner . . .**

and, dare I even say it . . .

CLOWNS!

It's my job to keep us safe from such perils.

Like making everyone aware that sliding down banisters is very dangerous business.

But no one listens to me. We could lose a tooth or something! **Is it worth it, people?**

It's a thankless job. Somebody's gotta do it. But let me tell you what I do like....

I like SAFETY!

I like being surrounded by soft things, like feathers and marshmallows. Oh, and socks!

And I

LOVE

to relax in the evenings, sip a cup of tea, and watch a peaceful nature show. . . .

AHHH

HHHH!

Awww!
What a cute little hippo!